Presented To:

_____

From:

_____

On This Date:

_____

bible ✞ belles

truth becomes her

Books may be purchased by contacting the publisher Truth Becomes Her, at hello@truthbecomesher.com

Published in San Diego, California by Truth Becomes Her. Bible Belles and Truth Becomes Her are registered trademarks.

This book was created as a result of hard work, prayers, coffee, prayers, a lot of late nights, prayers, so much help from others, prayers, and a whole bunch of God's grace. Did we mention prayers?

Illustrations by: Megan Crisp

Interior Design by: John Trent

Cover Design by: Ron Eddy and Megan Crisp

Editing by: Julie Breihan

Printed in the United States

ISBN: 978-0-9961689-5-3

The Adventures of Rooney Cruz

Deborah
The Belle of Leadership

written by
Erin Weidemann

illustrated by
Megan Crisp

Welcome, Little Belle.

Your superhero journey
begins right now…

"Arise and look up toward the sky.

Warriors, lift your banners high!"

Rooney looked around the auditorium as the students sang. Today was the last dress rehearsal for *Word Warriors*, this year's school play, and the room was buzzing with excitement. She and her classmates had practiced for months, and tonight was the big night.

Rooney turned to her partner, Jaden. "Are you ready for tonight?" she asked. "I can't believe it's finally here!"

"I guess so." Jaden shrugged. "It just feels kind of weird with all you girls not talking to each other."

Rooney's eyes moved up the aisles and across rows of empty chairs. Her friend Dani was sitting in the last row with Kylie, Maddie, and a few other girls. Then Dani looked up.

The two girls locked eyes. Rooney smiled warmly, but Dani quickly turned her head.

Rooney touched each of the bells dangling from her wrist. She lifted her head. *God, we've got this*, she prayed. *I know You will help me figure this out.*

Just then her teacher, Mrs. McLean, stood up. "All right, everybody, it's time to take a break. Stay in your costumes and head out to the playground. We'll finish the rehearsal when you come back from recess."

As she rose to walk outside, Rooney felt a rumbling beneath her feet.

"Coming through!"

Dani and the rest of the Back-Row Girls stampeded down the main aisle, pushing their way to the front of the line.

"Watch it!"

"Owww. Wait your turn!" A few of Rooney's classmates snapped back at them.

It was a big mess as all of the students tried to shove past each other.

"Enough!"

Mrs. McLean scolded. "We are hours away from our big show and this is how you choose to behave?"

She held out her hands. "Now, let's try it again. One at a time."

The students walked single file out the door. Rooney waited until they had all gone. She stood there, looking at the bells on her wrist.

God, she prayed, *we've worked so hard for months now. We need Your help to work together. Help us make this play the absolute best it can be.*

Rooney walked outside and sat down under her favorite tree. Moments later, she heard a faint buzzing sound. She looked up and saw a bumblebee circling above her head.

"You know, bees are really amazing creatures."

Rooney stood up quickly. "Mari! I had a feeling I'd see you today."

The angel giggled. "Well, I couldn't wait! I'm so excited to see your play. You and your classmates have worked so hard memorizing lines and learning the movements."

Rooney nodded. "I just wish we were getting along better. Dani still isn't speaking to me. She and the other girls are kind of ignoring the rest of us."

"Come here, you little cutie."

Mari held out her hands. The tiny bee hovered above them. It settled down inside the angel's palms, fluttering its wings.

"You know, bees have short lives, but their work is very important. Each of them has a special job to do. It's no coincidence that this beauty is buzzing above your head today, Rooney. God has a special job for you too."

"He does?"

Mari raised her hands. "Yeah!"

The bee lifted off and continued to fly circles in the air. Mari looked at Rooney.

"It's time for you to meet Deborah."

"Deborah. Cool! Is she a Bible Belle too?"

"Yes. She was Israel's first and only female judge. She led her people to win a great and glorious battle. Oh," Mari sang happily, "and her name means 'bee.'"

Rooney's eyes lit up. "All right, Mari! Let's do it."

"Can I see your bracelet?" Mari wiggled in the air.

Rooney held out her arm. The little angel placed her hands on Rooney's wrist. The golden bracelet began to glow. Brighter and brighter, it glowed until a burst of light revealed a wide, wooden window.

Rooney grinned. "I love it when that happens."

"So," Mari explained, "Deborah was the leader of Israel during this time. She was a prophet and a judge, and the people would come to her for help and advice."

"Is that her?" Rooney pointed to a woman sitting underneath the large fronds of a tall palm tree.

"Yep. Back then, not many women had that kind of responsibility, so it was a pretty big deal. Anyway, in those days the people of Israel were ruled by the Canaanites. The captain of the Canaanite army was a powerful man named Sisera." Mari pointed over the hill.

"Sisera?" Rooney leaned in to take a closer look.

"These guys ruled over God's people for twenty years. Finally, they had had enough. That's when Deborah sprang into action."

Rooney watched as Deborah gave an order to a soldier standing nearby. "I want to speak to Barak, the commander of our army. Send him to me."

After a few minutes, Rooney watched a man make his way up to Deborah's palm tree. "You wanted to see me?"

Deborah stood up. "The Lord, the God of Israel, commands you: 'Go, take ten thousand of our men and lead them up to Mount Tabor. I will lead our enemy, Sisera, and his army to the river and give them into your hands.'"

Barak stared at Deborah. "If you go with me," he finally said, "I will go. But if you don't go with me, then I won't go."

"Wait." Rooney scratched her head. "He's the guy in charge of the army. Did he just say he's not going to lead the men into battle unless Deborah goes with him?"

Mari flew up and landed on Rooney's shoulder. "Absolutely. Barak is afraid, but Deborah knows that God's people will win the battle. She's going to do her part to see it done."

"Certainly I will go with you," Deborah agreed. "But because of the choice you are making, the honor in this fight will not be yours. The Lord will deliver Sisera into the hands of a woman."

All of a sudden the window shook. Rooney could see Barak and his soldiers gathered together.

Mari whispered, "When Sisera finds out that Barak's army has gone up the mountain, he calls for his men to attack."

Rooney looked back through the window. She could see Deborah, standing proudly at the top of the hill.

Rooney watched as Deborah gave orders to Barak. "Go!" Deborah shouted. "This is the day the Lord has given Sisera into your hands. Do not be afraid!"

She raised her sword. "God has gone ahead of you, and He will protect you!"

Chariots thundered across the land.

Soldiers on both sides raced toward each other. A great cloud of dust filled the air. Rooney could hear the clanging of swords and the clashing of armor.

Her eyes searched the countryside. A short while later, the dust settled back to the ground. Finally, she could see that Israel's soldiers were the ones left standing.

"He's getting away!" Rooney watched as Sisera jumped down from his chariot and took off running.

"Don't worry about him." Mari shook her head. "Remember how Deborah said that Sisera would be delivered into a woman's hands? Well, her name is Jael. She's going to take it from here."

Rooney jumped into the air.

"Mari, that's amazing! God was on their side. Deborah knew it, and they won!"

"That's right. Deborah led a successful attack against the forces of Sisera, the Canaanites, and their army. She became known as a great leader, the warrior who inspired her people and led them to victory."

Rooney looked back through the window. Deborah and Barak were standing among the soldiers, celebrating and singing together.

"Israel's leaders took charge, and the people gladly followed. Praise the Lord!"

Mari flew down and held Rooney's hand.

"Rooney, in your life you will face many difficult battles. Being a leader is more than having the wisdom to know what needs to be done. A true leader is able to stir action in herself and others. That's what Deborah did."

Mari continued. "Deborah loved and trusted God. She devoted her life to doing the work He created her to do. That's what it means to be a leader. It's having a strong faith, a willing heart, and a life dedicated to love, sacrifice, and service."

Rooney listened as Deborah and Barak sang.

"So may all your enemies perish, Lord! But may all who love you be like the sun when it rises in its strength."

Rooney hugged Mari, and her eyes filled with happy tears.

"God wants you to lead, Rooney."

Mari spun her hands in the air, faster and faster, until a bright, shining bell appeared.

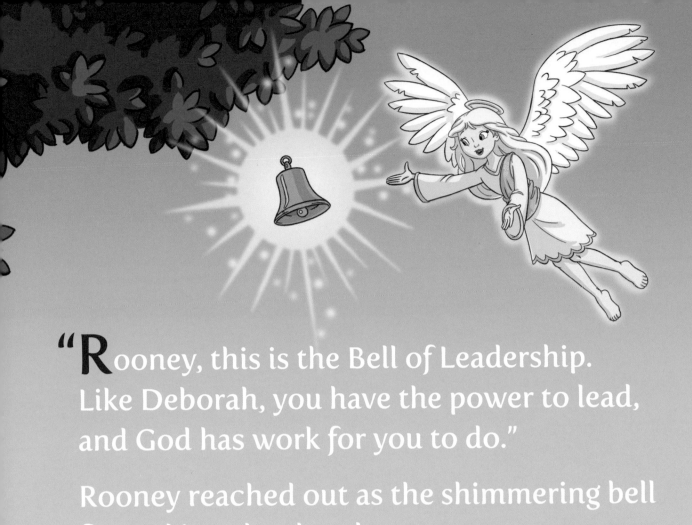

"Rooney, this is the Bell of Leadership. Like Deborah, you have the power to lead, and God has work for you to do."

Rooney reached out as the shimmering bell floated into her hands.

Mari hovered in the air. "God created every girl to have a voice that matters. That includes you."

"God wants me to use my voice? How?"

"Loop in that bell and find out."

Rooney opened the clasp on the bracelet and attached the new bell. That's when it happened— the five letters on the bells began to glow. Rooney's eyes widened. She read the letters aloud.

"H–E–A–R–D," she whispered. "Heard."

"The world is loud, Rooney, and it has a lot to say about the kind of girl you should be. But God made you strong and He gave you a powerful voice. He created you to battle back against the noise of this world."

Mari glided back and forth above Rooney's head. "God made you to be heard, to use your voice for Him."

The bracelet floated into the air. Rooney listened as, one by one, the shimmering bells began to ring.

"Rooney, this is what it means to be a Bible Belle. She is a girl who does not follow the crowd."

Mari flew closer. "She is a girl who makes a different kind of noise."

"Wow. That's amazing!"

Rooney's eyes were wide open. She took the glowing bracelet and fastened it around her wrist.

Rooney closed her eyes.

"God, I'm ready," she declared. "I know what You made me to do. You made me like Hannah. I can talk to You, and I know You're always listening. I am like Esther. You prepare my heart and help me to be ready for the right time to act."

She grasped her wrist. "You made me like Abigail. I am brave enough to do the right things because You are always with me. You made me like Ruth. I can love others faithfully and put their needs before my own. You made me like Deborah. I can be a leader."

She lifted her arms into the air. "Please show me how You want me to lead."

Later that night, Rooney stood in front of her bedroom mirror. She looked at her reflection.

"God," she prayed, "for a long time I didn't really know myself. A lot of the time I was scared and confused. I understand now."

She touched the glowing bells that dangled from her wrist.

"Thank You for these powers. I'm going to use them, and I will start tonight. I can be the leader You made me to be."

"Well, of course you can." Rooney whipped around. Her mom was standing in the doorway. "You almost ready to go?" She gave her a wink.

"Be right there," Rooney said, smiling. She grabbed her costume and raced downstairs.

The lights and decorations were all in place. The auditorium was alive with crowds of people. Rooney walked down to the stage door. Jaden was there, sitting on the ground.

Rooney tapped her on the shoulder. "Hey, do you want to practice our lines while we get ready?"

Jaden grinned. "Sure. I wasn't nervous earlier today, but now it feels like there's a dance party in my stomach."

They found a little corner backstage. Most of their classmates joined them. When she looked up, Rooney noticed Dani and the other girls sitting against the wall.

God, no matter what happens, I know You're with me, Rooney prayed as she walked over to the girls.

"Do you want to come over and practice with us?" Rooney asked. The girls pretended not to hear.

"Listen," Rooney continued, her voice strong and steady, "we can't let the trouble between us get in the way of our performance tonight. Everyone has worked so hard to make this play awesome."

Maddie rolled her eyes. "Rooney, why do you always have to make everything about you?"

"This is not about me," Rooney said calmly. "It's about all of us. We are a team. Each of us brings something special to this play. We can do this, but we have to do it together."

The girls looked at her. After a few moments, Dani stood up.

"Rooney's right," she said. "Tonight will be a disaster if we don't work together."

"Wait here." Rooney ran back over to the practice group. "Come on, everyone. Let's make this the best performance ever."

The group gathered together. Rooney clenched her fist and reached for the middle of the circle. One at a time, each student put a hand in.

"Are all of my Word Warriors ready?"
Mrs. McLean asked.

The students moved into their first positions,
but Rooney held back for a moment.

"Almost. I just need a second."

She walked over to Dani. "Thanks for standing
up for me back there. I hope you know that I
love you and I'm still your friend. I hate that
we are fighting, and I miss you."

Dani was quiet for a minute.

"I miss you too."

"You miss me?"

"Yeah. The other girls, well, I can't talk to them like I talk to you. Can you forgive me for being so mean to you?"

Rooney didn't hesitate. "Yes, of course I forgive you." Rooney gave Dani a big hug.

A leader loves, she thought.
A leader forgives.

Just then their teacher clapped her hands.

"Show time!"

"Stand up, stand tall upon the Word. Warrior, let your voice be heard!"

At the end of the play, the curtain closed. The audience erupted in applause. As the students lined up, Dani squeezed Rooney's hand.

"Hey," Dani asked as they took their bows, "where did you get that awesome bracelet?"

Rooney looked up at Mari. A warm wave came over her. She smiled.

She knew that a much greater adventure was about to begin.

So humble
yourselves under
the mighty power
of God, and at the
right time he
will lift you
up in honor.

— I Peter 5:6